STAR WARS

FINN & REY ESCAPE!

Written by
MICHAEL SIGLAIN

Illustrated by
BRIAN ROOD

© & TM 2015 Lucasfilm Ltd. All rights reserved.

Published by Disney • Lucasfilm Press, an imprint of Disney Book Group. No part of this book may be reproduced or transmitted in any form or by any means, electronic or mechanical, including photocopying, recording, or by any information storage and retrieval system, without written permission from the publisher. For information address Disney • Lucasfilm Press, 1101 Flower Street, Glendale, California 91201.

Printed in the United States of America

First Edition, December 2015

1 3 5 7 9 10 8 6 4 2

Library of Congress Control Number on file

FAC-029261-15306

ISBN 978-1-4847-0479-0

ISBN 978-1-4847-5861-8

Visit the official *Star Wars* website at: www.starwars.com.

SUSTAINABLE
FORESTRY
INITIATIVE
Certified Sourcing
www.sfiprogram.org
SFI-01415

Disney
LUCASFILM
PRESS

Los Angeles · New York

On the sandy planet of Jakku lived a lonely girl named **Rey**.

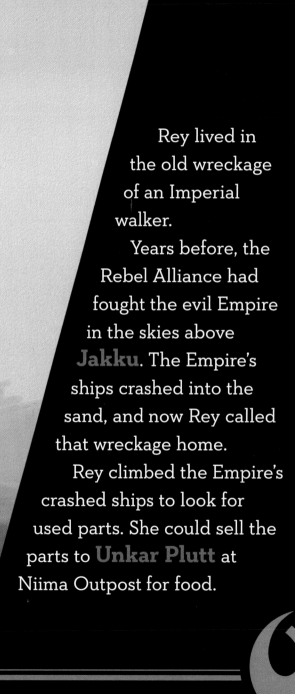

Rey lived in the old wreckage of an Imperial walker.

Years before, the Rebel Alliance had fought the evil Empire in the skies above **Jakku**. The Empire's ships crashed into the sand, and now Rey called that wreckage home.

Rey climbed the Empire's crashed ships to look for used parts. She could sell the parts to **Unkar Plutt** at Niima Outpost for food.

One day, Rey saw a **small droid** caught in a net. It was up to Rey to save the droid.

The droid, named **BB-8**, followed Rey wherever she went. Rey thought about selling BB-8 to Unkar Plutt, but she soon changed her mind. She liked BB-8 too much to sell him.

Unkar was mad at Rey for not selling him BB-8. He sent some of
his **thugs** to steal the droid. But Rey used her staff to stop them.
What Rey didn't know was that someone was watching her. . . .

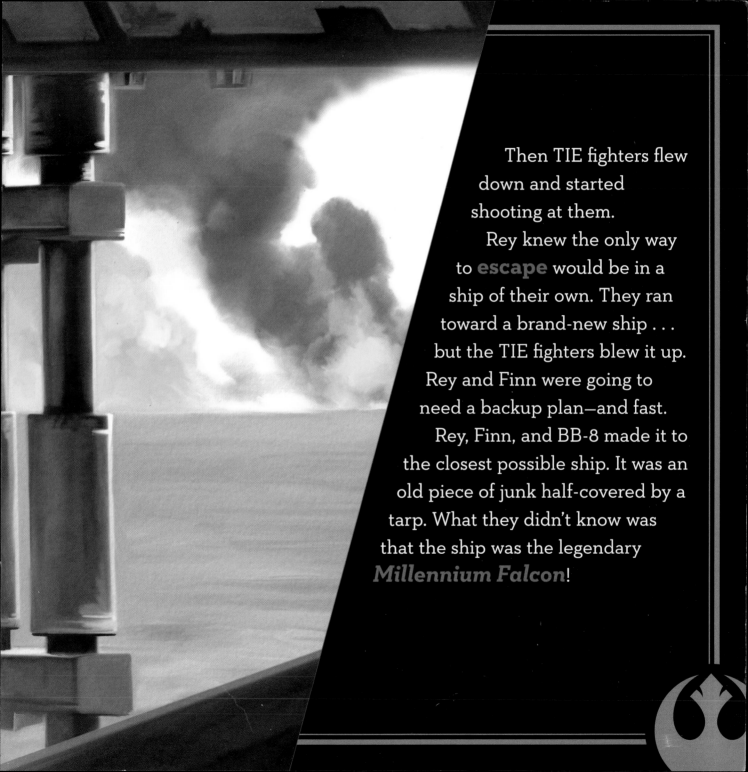

Then TIE fighters flew down and started shooting at them.

Rey knew the only way to **escape** would be in a ship of their own. They ran toward a brand-new ship . . . but the TIE fighters blew it up. Rey and Finn were going to need a backup plan—and fast.

Rey, Finn, and BB-8 made it to the closest possible ship. It was an old piece of junk half-covered by a tarp. What they didn't know was that the ship was the legendary *Millennium Falcon*!

Rey immediately ran into the cockpit and sat in the captain's chair. She turned on the engines and the old ship lurched forward.

The *Millennium Falcon* rose through a cloud of sand and smoke. It **rocketed away** from Niima, but the TIE fighters gave chase. The enemy ships fired on the *Falcon*. Rey quickly thought of a way to lose them.

Rey piloted the *Millennium Falcon* through the **spaceship graveyard**! All but one of the TIE fighters crashed. The last one dodged the wreckage and wouldn't stop firing at the *Falcon*.

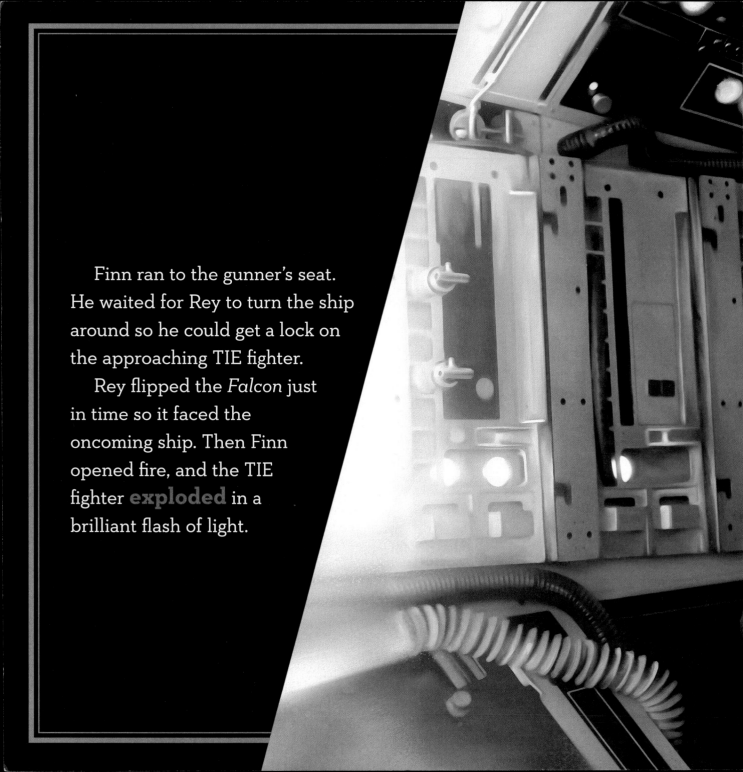

Finn ran to the gunner's seat. He waited for Rey to turn the ship around so he could get a lock on the approaching TIE fighter.

Rey flipped the *Falcon* just in time so it faced the oncoming ship. Then Finn opened fire, and the TIE fighter **exploded** in a brilliant flash of light.

As Rey and Finn escaped from Jakku in the *Millennium Falcon*, Finn told Rey all about BB-8. She agreed to help Finn return the droid to the Resistance. Rey and Finn knew that their **adventures** had only just begun.

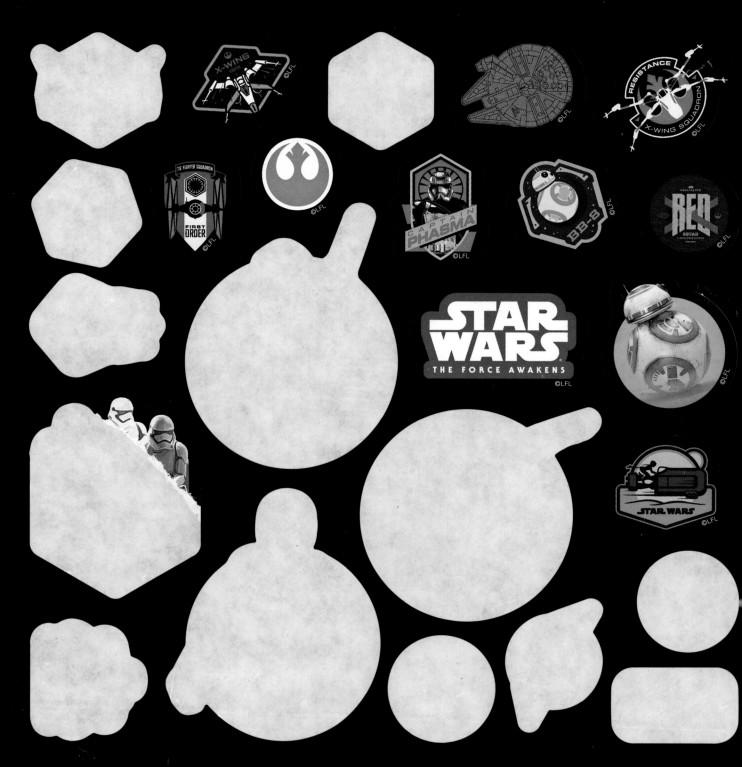

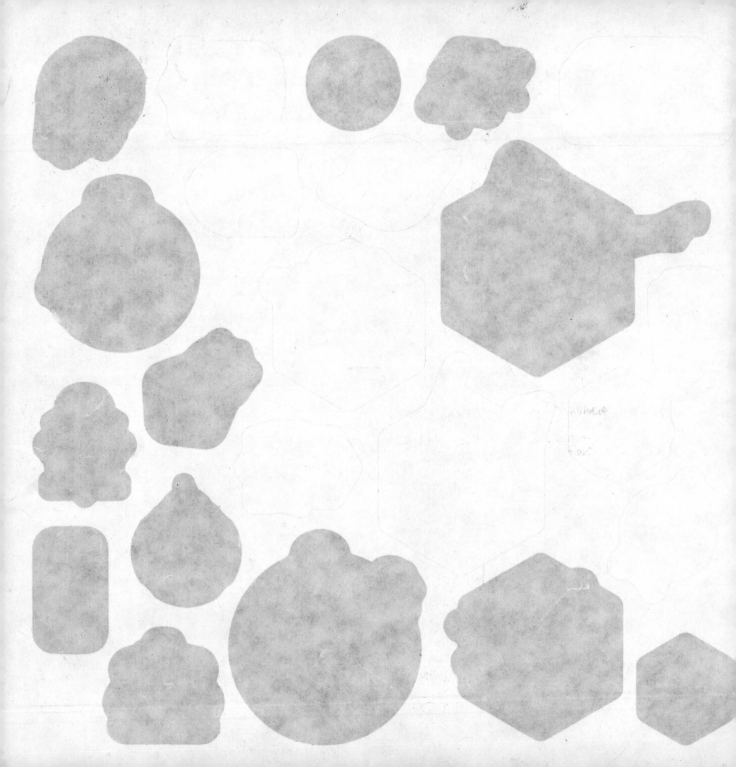